This book
belongs to

Annie

Smith

ORCHARD BOOKS

First published in Great Britain in 2016 by The Watts Publishing Group

1 3 5 7 9 10 8 6 4 2

HASBRO and its logo, MY LITTLE PONY and all related characters are
trademarks of Hasbro and are used with permission.

© 2016 Hasbro. All rights reserved.

A CIP catalogue record for this book is available from the British Library

ISBN 978 1 40834 145 2

Printed and bound in China

Orchard Books
An imprint of Hachette Children's Group
Part of The Watts Publishing Group Limited
Carmelite House
50 Victoria Embankment
London EC4Y 0DZ

An Hachette UK Company
www.hachette.co.uk

www.hachettechildrens.co.uk

Adult supervision is recommended for all
baking and cooking activities, and when
glue, paint, scissors and other
sharp points are in use.

Contents

Welcome!

Hello friend, we're so pleased to see you! Inside this book, we will take you on a VIP (Very Important Pony!) tour of our magical kingdom, Equestria. As we explore, there'll be lots of activities and games, fantastic facts, sparkling stories, sensational stickers and heaps of My Little Pony magic!

So, what are we waiting for? Let's have an EPIC adventure!

Love and hugs,

Twilight Sparkle, Rainbow Dash, Pinkie Pie, Fluttershy, Rarity, Applejack (and Spike!)

xxxxxx

MAIL

Our World

Equestria is the most magical kingdom in the universe! It has a city in the clouds, towering mountains, a sparkling metropolis and the most beautiful castle ever. Here are some favourite friends to show you around.

Cloudsdale

Cloudsdale is a city in the sky! It's easiest for flying ponies like me and Fluttershy to visit this special place, as you need wings to get there.

CLOUDSDALE

CANTERLOT

PONYVILLE

EVERFREE

APPLEWOOD

Canterlot

Canterlot is the capital of Equestria. We rule the kingdom together from our home, Canterlot Castle. The castle is a truly magical place with more than 200 elegant rooms.

N

W E

S

Ponyville

Ponyville is home to me and my best friends. At the heart of the town is the square, where every pony gathers to hang out. There are also lots of shops, a school and a train station.

The Crystal Empire

The Crystal Empire is right at the top of Equestria. Made from millions of shining crystals, it's the most sparkling place in the kingdom!

CRYSTAL EMPIRE

Everfree Forest

Some ponies say that Everfree Forest is a bit spooky, but my animal friends and I really like living in our cosy cottage on the edge of the forest.

PLE LOOSA

Appleloosa

Appleloosa is a real old-fashioned Wild West town. My cousin, Braeburn, lives down there. When we visit him we always pay a visit to the saloon, the Salt Block, for some refreshments!

6 is the Magic Number!

No matter where you are in Equestria, these six best friends are at the heart of every adventure! Here's the low-down on these friendly fillies. Add a pretty sticker of each pony to the page.

© Hasbro

© Hasbro

Princess Twilight Sparkle hasn't always been a princess. Twilight's mentor, Princess Celestia, sent her to Ponyville to learn all about friendship. She did so well and helped so many ponies that she was crowned Equestria's newest princess!

Pinkie Pie is the most energetic pony in all of Ponyville. She just loves to have fun and make people laugh. She also bakes the most delicious cupcakes in all of Equestria. YUM!

Rarity is a glamorous and generous unicorn with a flair for fashion design! Every pony trots to her shop, the Carousel Boutique, for elegant outfits.

Fluttershy is a kind and timid Pegasus pony who loves animals and nature. Fluttershy is from Cloudsdale, but now she lives near Everfree Forest in a cute cottage.

Applejack lives with her large family on Sweet Apple Acres Farm. Honest and hardworking, Applejack is always busy but never forgets to make time for her family and friends.

Rainbow Dash is a speedy Pegasus pony who zooms through the skies! Although she's often on the move, loyal Rainbow Dash is never too busy to spend time with her friends.

CAPITAL CANTERLOT

Canterlot is the capital city of Equestria!

Fabulous features: This beautiful city features tall ivory towers with golden spires, and has many rivers and waterfalls running through it.

Exciting events: Canterlot hosts many of Equestria's most fabulous social events, including the Grand Galloping Gala and the Canterlot Garden Party.

Train travels: It takes about a day to travel from Ponyville to Canterlot on the train, although it's much quicker if you can fly!

Royal wedding! Canterlot Castle, where Princess Celestia and Princess Luna live, was the venue for the wonderful wedding of Princess Cadance and Prince Shining Armor.

Castle Colouring

Canterlot Castle is the jewel in the crown of the capital city! Can you use your colouring pens and pencils to make this castle shine? Then use your stickers to add prince and princess ponies to the scene.

© Hasbro

Spike's Sparkly Search

Oh no! Spike has lost eight precious gems in Ponyville. Can you help him find them all? You'll have to look carefully. Give yourself a sparkly heart sticker when you've spotted them all.

I've found them all!

Turn to page 62 for the answers

IN THE PONY KNOW

The My Little Pony friends are always having amazing adventures! Test your knowledge by trying to correctly answer these questions. Award yourself a pretty flower sticker for every answer you get right.

1

Pinkie Pie discovered a magic pool in Everfree Forest. What happened each time she walked into the pool?

A She got wet!

B Another Pinkie Pie appeared

C A naughty fish nibbled her hoof

2

Princess Cadance and Prince Shining Armor had a wonderful wedding planned. Which rotten royal tried their best to ruin the special occasion?

A Princess Celestia

B Queen Chrysalis

C King Sombra

4

When the Crystal Empire was due to host the Equestria Games, who did Twilight Sparkle and her friends try their best to impress?

A Spike

B Princess Luna

C The official Games Inspector

3

Apple Bloom, Scootaloo and Sweetie Belle are the very best of friends. But what are these three young ponies missing?

A Their cutie marks

B Their tails

C Their voices!

5

What little creatures did poor Fluttershy find herself having to look after when they got stuck in Ponyville?

A Sneezies

B Breezies

C Kneezies

Turn to page 62 for the answers.

Put your stickers here!

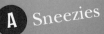

15

RAINBOW DASH'S RIGHT-START RECIPES!

Rainbow Dash is always on the move, so she needs a yummy and healthy breakfast to help her zoom around the skies! You'll need a bit of help from a grown-up with these recipes.

Brilliant Banana Smoothie

1. Put all the ingredients into a blender.

2. Ask a grown-up to help you put the lid on the blender, and then blend for about 30 seconds.

3. Pour into a tall glass and enjoy!

Makes one large smoothie

INGREDIENTS

200ml milk

One banana

One teaspoon of honey

Three tablespoons of oats

Cheeky Cheese Muffins

INGREDIENTS

1 large egg

100ml milk

250g grated mature cheddar cheese

125g self-raising flour

1 teaspoon paprika

½ teaspoon of mustard (or mustard powder)

A little bit of butter or margarine (for greasing muffin tin/ moulds)

You will also need a muffin tin or muffin moulds

1. Ask a grown-up to preheat the oven to 200C/ gas mark 6.

2. Beat the egg in a bowl, then add the milk.

3. Put the flour, paprika, cheese and mustard into another bowl and mix together.

4. Add the egg and milk to the flour mixture and fold in gently (don't worry – the mixture is supposed to be lumpy!)

5. Grease your muffin tin or muffin moulds with a little bit of butter. Spoon the mixture into the muffin tin.

6. Ask a grown-up to put the muffins into the oven. Bake for 12–15 minutes until firm and golden brown.

7. Once cooked, ask a grown-up to take the muffins from the oven and allow to cool for a few minutes. Then remove from the tin and enjoy!

RARITY
TAKES MANEHATTAN

RARITY WAS VERY EXCITED. SHE WAS GOING TO VISIT THE **CITY OF MANEHATTAN** TO TAKE PART IN **FASHION WEEK**! BEST OF ALL, HER FRIENDS WERE GOING WITH HER. RARITY HAD EVEN MANAGED TO GET TICKETS FOR THE HOTTEST MUSICAL IN TOWN, **HINNY OF THE HILLS**!

WHEN THEY GOT TO MANEHATTAN, THE FRIENDS THOUGHT THAT EVERYPONY WAS **VERY BUSY** AND **QUITE GRUMPY**. BUT **RARITY** WAS DETERMINED TO MAKE THE MANEHATTAN PONIES SMILE BY SHOWING LOTS OF KINDNESS AND GENEROSITY.

THE **WINNER OF FASHION WEEK** WOULD HAVE THEIR DRESSES DISPLAYED IN THE FANCIEST SHOPS IN MANEHATTAN.

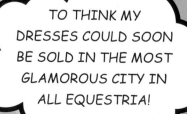

TO THINK MY DRESSES COULD SOON BE SOLD IN THE MOST GLAMOROUS CITY IN ALL EQUESTRIA!

RARITY NEEDED TO BE AT THE RUNWAY BY TWO O'CLOCK TO ENTER HER DESIGNS FOR THE COMPETITION. MAKING IT JUST IN TIME, SHE BUMPED INTO A PONY SHE USED TO KNOW, CALLED SURI. RARITY KINDLY GAVE SURI A PIECE OF HER VERY SPECIAL FABRIC.

LATER ON THAT DAY, **RARITY** WAS HORRIFIED TO SEE THAT SURI HAD USED THE FABRIC TO CREATE TOTALLY **NEW DESIGNS FOR HERSELF!**

YOU STOLE MY IDEAS! HOW COULD YOU POSSIBLY MAKE NEW OUTFITS SO FAST?

SURI TOLD **RARITY** THAT HER ASSISTANT, **MISS POMMEL**, HAD MADE ALL THE NEW DESIGNS FOR HER. RARITY **LEFT THE RUNWAY IN TEARS.**

IT'S EVERY PONY FOR HERSELF IN THE BIG CITY, SWEETIE!

BACK AT THE HOTEL, THE OTHER PONIES COULDN'T WAIT TO SEE **HINNY OF THE HILLS.** THEN RARITY EXPLAINED WHAT HAD HAPPENED. SHE WISHED SHE'D NEVER GIVEN SURI THE PIECE OF FABRIC!

MY GENEROSITY HAS RUINED ME!

BUT RARITY'S FRIENDS WERE THERE TO HELP.

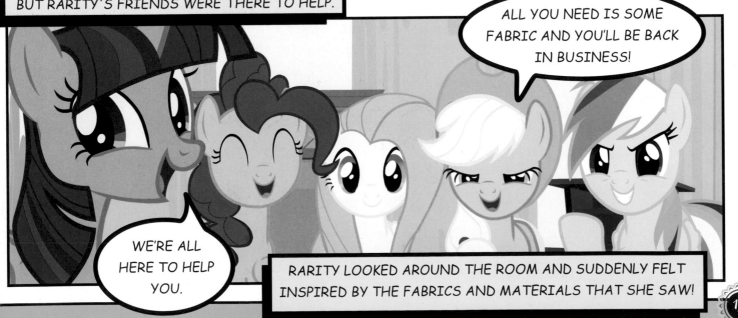

ALL YOU NEED IS SOME FABRIC AND YOU'LL BE BACK IN BUSINESS!

WE'RE ALL HERE TO HELP YOU.

RARITY LOOKED AROUND THE ROOM AND SUDDENLY FELT INSPIRED BY THE FABRICS AND MATERIALS THAT SHE SAW!

THE **PONIES** AND **SPIKE** WORKED THROUGH THE NIGHT TO HELP RARITY MAKE HER NEW DESIGNS. THEY MISSED DINNER AND **HINNY OF THE HILLS**. THEY HOPED **RARITY** WOULD BE GRATEFUL, BUT SHE DIDN'T EVEN SAY **THANK YOU!**

RARITY MADE IT TO THE RUNWAY JUST IN TIME WITH HER NEW COLLECTION, 'HOTEL CHIC'. EVERYONE LOVED IT! BUT RARITY REALISED THAT THE ONLY PONIES SHE CARED ABOUT WEREN'T IN THE AUDIENCE . . . SHE'D TREATED HER FRIENDS SO BADLY THAT THEY HADN'T COME TO THE SHOW.

RARITY LEFT THE SHOW EARLY AND WENT TO FIND HER FRIENDS. SHE DIDN'T KNOW THAT THEY HADN'T MEANT TO MISS HER SHOW; THEY'D JUST OVERSLEPT BECAUSE THEY WERE SO TIRED AFTER WORKING ALL NIGHT!

LATER THAT DAY, **MISS POMMEL** TOLD **RARITY** THAT SHE HAD **WON THE FIRST PRIZE TROPHY** FOR FASHION WEEK! RARITY WAS DELIGHTED TO HAVE WON, BUT SHE ALREADY FELT LIKE A WINNER KNOWING SHE HAD THE BEST FRIENDS **EVER!**

THE END

FASHION INSPIRATION!

Rarity was inspired by Manehattan to create her 'Hotel Chic' collection. Can you use your stickers to give Rarity and Miss Pommel magnificent Manehattan-style makeovers? Let your imagination run wild!

POW!!

21

Where in the World?

If you were to live in Equestria, where would be the perfect place for YOU? Answer the questions in this quiz to find out!

Describe your perfect view

A A forest glade

B An elegant city, shining in the sun

C A gorgeous sky full of sun, clouds and rainbows!

D A small town full of friendly faces

Which of these places sounds the best to you?

A A cosy home full of friends

B A stylish residence with lots of rooms

C An outdoor home with a dramatic view

D A peaceful place with space to be creative

MOSTLY As

Your ideal home is Fluttershy's cottage. You love animals and would fit in perfectly in this happy home on the edge of Everfree Forest.

MOSTLY Bs

Your perfect place is Canterlot Castle, alongside Princess Celestia and Princess Luna. This royal residence with its elegant rooms and gardens would suit you perfectly.

What time do you like to get up in the mornings?

A You're always up when the sun rises to look after your animal friends

B You have to get up early to fit in all your social engagements!

C You're so active during the day that a little lie-in is always welcome . . .

D Lying under the duvet with a book is your favourite way to spend a morning

What is your bedroom like?

A It's filled with pictures of animals and friends

B Elegant and very tidy

C A bit of a mess, but it has a super-comfy bed!

D Cosy, with lots of books

What is your favourite food?

A A delicious salad with lots of nuts and seeds

B A classic Victoria sponge

C Something you can eat on the go, like a smoothie or a tasty muffin

D A yummy pie or warming soup

MOSTLY Cs

You're suited for living the high life up in Cloudsdale! You're so active and fun-loving that you're sure to be besties with the Pegasus ponies who live in this amazing place.

MOSTLY Ds

The gorgeous Golden Oak Library in Ponyville is where you would feel right at home. This friendly place is just perfect for a book lover. Princess Twilight Sparkle and Spike can't wait to welcome you!

HOW TO DRAW... SPIKE THE DRAGON

Spike the Dragon is Twilight Sparkle's closest pal and loyal assistant. Show off your creative side by learning how to recreate the cutest dragon in Equestria. Use a pencil to do all the stages at first, and you'll need a bit of help from a grown-up. Remember, practise makes perfect!

Step 1

Always use a pencil for this step. Start by drawing two separate circles. The top circle should be a little larger than the bottom one. Now add a line across the middle of the top circle.

Step 2

When you've practised a few times, you can use a pen from this stage on. Carefully add the outline of Spike's head, cheek and snout.

Step 3

Now Spike really starts to take shape! Add his distinctive head frill and his left ear tuft. Draw a line to connect the head circle together with the body circle.

Step 4

Next, add Spike's square-shaped eyes, making a thicker line at the top of each one for his eyelids. Then add a little hole on his nose and one small fang. Draw the small left line of Spike's mouth.

24

Step 5

Now add two curved lines above Spike's eyes for eyebrows. Draw two thick vertical lines inside the eyes, and a curved line for eyeballs. Draw one more line from the back of the nose down to the bottom of the head circle. This makes the other side of Spike's mouth.

Step 6

Now it's time to start creating Spike's body! Add a curved line for his chest and draw his two little arms and hands. At the back of the neck, draw a curved line showing the start of Spike's back.

Step 7

Draw Spike's pointed tail and then add legs and feet. Don't worry if it's not perfectly neat, remember, practise really does make perfect!

Step 8

Now it's time to add those finishing touches. Add frills to Spike's tail, and lines to his tummy and chest. Then carefully rub out the pencil circles you drew in step 1.

YOU'VE DONE IT!

Spike is ready to colour in. Using your stickers, surround your picture of Spike with some precious treasure!

my LiTTLE PONY

25

Exploring Everfree Forest

Everfree Forest may be a mysterious and magical place, but it's also home to many creatures! Can you add lots of stickers to this scene? Don't forget to add friendly Fluttershy, plus her animal pals and some birds and butterflies.

© Hasbro

© Hasbro

Fabulous Future

The My Little Ponies know that each of us is in charge of our own destiny, but they still love a sneaky peek at their ponyscopes! What do the months ahead hold for YOU?

AQUARIUS
(21st Jan – 19th Feb)

You are creative, clever and independent. This year holds an exciting new project for you – perhaps you have a craft idea to develop or a special story you'd like to write.

ARIES
(21st March – 20th April)

You are energetic, strong and affectionate. There's an exciting opportunity to join a new team in the coming months, so keep your eyes open!

PISCES
(20th Feb – 20th March)

Your friends would say you are sensitive, smiley and a bit of a dreamer. An animal will feature in your year ahead – perhaps you'll help look after a new pet at home or school?

GEMINI
(22nd May – 21st June)

You are curious, active and love to be on the move! Your creativity will be needed for a special project soon. Perhaps you already have an art project in mind . . . ?

TAURUS
(21st April – 21st May)

You are kind, gentle and always have time for your loved ones. You'll make a special new friend this year who you'll have lots of fun with!

CANCER
(22nd June – 23rd July)

You are loving and caring, and happiest when outside in a garden or park. An interesting nature project needs your help in the next few months.

LEO
(24th July – 23rd Aug)

You are happy, outgoing and playful! You're always leader of the pack. Your people skills will come in useful with a new drama project.

VIRGO
(24th Aug – 23rd Sept)

Your friends and family know you to be inquisitive and a perfectionist! You love books, and a fun opportunity with a creative writing project may come your way.

SCORPIO
(24th Oct – 22nd Nov)

You're very strong and full of energy. A new sporting event will challenge you and channel your amazing energy in new and exciting ways.

LIBRA
(24th Sept – 23rd Oct)

You're so sociable and love to be with your friends and family. There'll be an opportunity to plan a super-fun party very soon. What party themes can you think of?

SAGITTARIUS
(23rd Nov – 23rd Dec)

You are confident, happy and full of fun. An exciting school project will be happening soon, and you are the person to give it the magic and sparkle it needs!

CAPRICORN
(23rd Dec – 20th Jan)

You are very organised and imaginative. These skills will come in handy for a big group get-together or playdate in the near future.

HEY THERE, PONY PALS!

You're old pals with the main ponies, but have you been properly introduced to these other residents of Equestria?

PRINCESS CADANCE AND PRINCE SHINING ARMOR

Princess Cadance used to foal-sit for Twilight Sparkle when she was little! This gentle mare is married to Twilight's brother, Prince Shining Armor. Shining Armor is Captain of the Canterlot Royal Guard. He is brave and kind, but he can be stern at times.

BIG MAC AND GRANNY SMITH

Big Mac is Applejack's older brother, and Granny Smith is Applejack's and Big Mac's grandmother. Big Mac is very strong and does lots of the heavy work around the farm. He also has a very good singing voice! Granny Smith makes the most delicious apple pie.

MR AND MRS CAKE

These two friendly ponies own Ponville's bakery, Sugarcube Corner. They are the best bakers in town! They just love Pinkie Pie and are very patient with her, even when she eats their cakes and throws parties in the bakery.

BABS SEED

Babs Seed was the fourth member of the Cutie Mark Crusaders until she got her cutie mark. This little pony comes from Manehattan and is Apple Bloom's cousin.

SNIPS AND SNAILS

These two little unicorns are the best of friends. Snips is very kind and can be a bit dopey at times. Snails is a good student, and his long legs mean he's great at galloping!

DIAMOND TIARA AND SILVER SPOON

These young fillies can be a bit mean and snooty. They made the Cutie Mark Crusaders very upset when they teased them for not having their cutie marks. They are a tricky twosome to avoid!

Twilight Sparkle teaches you some new magic! MOVE FORWARD TWO SPACES

Uh-oh! Your spell has gone wrong! MISS A TURN

At school, Diamond Tiara is showing off! MOVE BACK THREE SPACES

Being friends with Princess Twilight Sparkle makes you the most popular pony in town! MOVE FORWARD FIVE SPACES

You hang out with old pal Pinkie Pie! MOVE FORWARD ONE SPACE

START!

HOW TO PLAY

Find Sweetie Belle, Scootaloo and Apple Bloom on the sticker sheet. Choose a character, then attach their sticker to a piece of card to make a counter. You'll also need a dice and at least one friend to play with. Throw the dice and take it in turns to move around the board. The first one to reach the end is the winner!

PRETTY PONYVILLE

Welcome to Pretty Ponyville!

The place to be: Lots of Ponyville action takes place at the town square. This is where Mayor Mare gives her speeches, the weekly market is held here and Princess Celestia always makes important announcements by the town hall.

Town traditions: Each year the residents of Ponyville take part in a Winter Wrap-Up. The ponies work together to sweep away winter and prepare Ponyville for spring.

Learning lots: All young ponies in Ponyville have their lessons at the schoolhouse. They learn lots of subjects including spell-reading, scroll-writing, aerial gymnastics and the history of cutie marks.

Better Together

Oh no! These five friendly residents of Ponyville have been separated from their favourite things. Can you find the right sticker and put it next to each character?

This lucky pony has a whole orchard full of these fruits!

In Twilight's house there are shelves full of these!

Some dragons hoard their treasure, but this little dragon eats these precious gems.

Pinkie Pie loves to make and eat these treats!

This cuddly creature is Fluttershy's best buddy.

Turn to page 62 for the answers.

© Hasbro

It's YOUR Story!

The ponies know you LOVE stories, and they'd like your help to complete this tale. Ask a grown-up to help you read the story out loud, and use your stickers to fill in the blanks.

It was a beautiful day in Ponyville. Princess Twilight Sparkle

and  decided to visit Canterlot to pay a visit to

and . They were organising a

wonderful garden party at Canterlot Castle! They wanted to

give their guests lots of and

and .

Fluttershy and offered to help. They asked

to bake some , Rarity to

make some and to help

chase the clouds away!

Princess Twilight Sparkle decided to wear her most sparkly

for the part wore a special

bow tie! All the friends travelled to Canterlot Castle by

. But when they got there they saw

and had eaten all the !

OH NO!

Twilight Sparkle and all her friends worked together to chase away

and . They used their magic and lots of

hard work to make the garden look magical for the party. There were so

many floating in the air and even shooting

in the sky!

When all the guests arrived they said how beautiful

looked. It was the most magical evening with lots of dancing, games and

! The My Little Ponies had the best time EVER!

DRESS-UP TIME!

Princesses Celestia and Luna host the most wonderful events in the whole of Equestria! Can you help them to look their best for the Grand Galloping Gala? Colour in the pictures, then use stickers to make the sensational sisters look extra special.

PRINCESS celestia

Princess Luna

SKY-HIGH CLOUDSDALE

Cloudsdale hovers high above Equestria!

Up in the air: Magical Cloudsdale is a truly unique place. This stunning city sits on a huge fluffy cloud. It's much bigger than it looks, and it's quite easy to get lost!

Flying room only: You need to have wings to visit Cloudsdale, or you'd fall through the clouds! When Twilight Sparkle became a princess and grew her wings, she flew up for a special visit.

Weather watch: All of the weather in Equestria is made in Cloudsdale's weather factory.

On the move: Cloudsdale isn't always in the same place! It can drift around the skies of Equestria.

PEGASUS PICTURE

Cloudsdale is looking a little empty! Can you add some flying ponies to this lovely scene, as well as some clouds and rainbows?

PERFECT PONY EARS

There's nothing cuter than an adorable pair of animal ears! Make and wear these pony ears to show everyone just how much you love My Little Pony!

YOU WILL NEED

- A plastic headband (the thicker the better!)
- A sheet of felt in your chosen colour/s – match yours to your favourite pony's ears!
- Fabric glue
- Scissors
- Approximately 6 pins
- A4 piece of paper
- A pen
- A grown-up helper!

1. First, you need to make a paper template for your pony ears. Fold a piece of A4 paper in half.

2. Draw a horizontal line above the fold of the paper. The space between this line and the fold of the paper should be around the same width as your headband.

3. Draw the shape of your My Little Pony ear.

5. Repeat stages three and four for your second ear.

4. Ask a grown-up to help you cut out this ear shape through both sides of the paper, including the rectangular space at the bottom of your ear, and pin it to your piece of felt.

6. Ask a grown-up to help you cut out your ear shapes from the piece of felt.

7. When you have finished cutting out both your ear shapes, wrap one around one side of the headband. The rectangular space at the bottom of the ear shape should form the base of this wraparound.

8. Match the two sides of the ear together on either side of the headband. Hold these in place and ask an adult to help you apply fabric glue around the edges of the ear. Don't use too much!

9. Repeat steps seven and eight for your second ear.

YOUR EARS ARE FINISHED!

SAY, WHAT?!

The Equestria ponies sometimes say some very odd things! Luckily, your friend Pinkie Pie is here to translate some of the funnier phrases for you.

When Applejack says...

"Are you saying my mouth's making promises my legs can't keep?!"

She means . . .

"Are you accusing me of bragging?!"

HA HA!

HA!

HA!

HA HA!

When Spike says...

HA!

"I'm ALL dragon. RAAR!"

He means . . .

"I may be small, but I'm tough!"

HA!

HA

HA HA

When Twilight Sparkle says...

"Tough love, baby!"

She means . . .

"You may not want to hear this, but it's the truth!"

HA HA!

When Fluttershy says...

"I'd like to be a tree!"

She means . . .

Well . . . Fluttershy just feels like being a tree!

HA!

HA HA!

HA!

Friendly Fluttershy

Can you join the dots to create a gorgeous picture of Fluttershy? When you've finished, decorate the page with more hearts, flowers and butterflies.

POWER PONIES!

Twilight Sparkle was fast asleep when a rustling noise woke her up. Yawning sleepily, she saw Spike reading a comic book. "Spike, isn't it time you went to sleep?" Twilight Sparkle asked.

Spike explained that he was just getting to a particularly exciting bit in *Power Ponies*, his new comic book!

"We have to fix up Luna and Celestia's old castle tomorrow," Twilight Sparkle said kindly. Finally, Spike went to sleep, but only after he'd read a few more pages.

The next day, Twilight Sparkle and her friends were at the old castle, performing a truly magical makeover!

"Looking great, everyone!" Twilight called to her pony pals as they dashed around cleaning, tidying and decorating.

Spike offered to help, but Twilight said that they had everything under control. So the little dragon went off to catch up on the adventures of the Power Ponies. But when he read out the mysterious words written at the very back of the comic, something extraordinary happened – Spike was sucked into the pages!

As Twilight Sparkle and the other ponies came to see what was going on, the friends were suddenly sucked into the comic too! When he opened his eyes, Spike realised that they had been transported into the comic book world of Maretropolis. His friends had been transformed into the six Power Ponies, and Spike had become their clumsy assistant, Hum Drum. "The only way to get out of here is to defeat Mane-iac," Spike cried, pointing to a pony with a crazy mane and very scary eyes!

The ponies realised that they all had different superpowers which could help them defeat Mane-iac. Only Spike had no special powers. "I don't know what to do to help," he sighed sadly. "In the comic, Hum Drum is no use at all."

"Good job you're not really Hum Drum, then!" said Twilight Sparkle, comforting her friend.

Spike led the Power Ponies to Mane-iac's headquarters in an old shampoo factory. "Time to Power Pony up!" cried Applejack, as the doors to the factory opened.

But – oh no! – Mane-iac used her Hairspray Ray of Doom to freeze the Power Ponies in their tracks! Then she dragged the helpless ponies into her headquarters. Spike was the only one left who could help!

"What am I supposed to do? I'm useless!" worried Spike, as he crawled into Mane-iac's factory. He saw his poor pony friends in a cage, still frozen by the Hairspray Ray!

"You'll live just long enough to see me fire the instrument of your destruction!" cackled Mane-iac, revealing a giant hair drier machine. "This will turn every pony's mane completely wild, and Maretropolis will be destroyed. You shall be my first victims!" she cackled, turning the weapon to face the Power Ponies.

Spike realised he HAD to do something! "When my friends really need me I DO come through!" he cried, and he managed to turn the Hairspray Ray of Doom against Mane-iac's assistants, giving the Power Ponies time to escape and use their superpowers!

When Fluttershy saw Mane-iac being mean to a teeny-tiny firefly, she used her special superpower and transformed into a huge monster! As monster Fluttershy destroyed the hair drier doomsday machine, a ray of power hit Mane-iac.

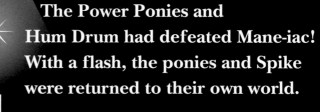

The Power Ponies and Hum Drum had defeated Mane-iac! With a flash, the ponies and Spike were returned to their own world.

"We wouldn't have made it without you, Spike," said Twilight Sparkle.

"I guess you don't need to have superpowers to be a super friend," said Spike.

And with that, the seven best friends headed home to Ponyville.

IMPRESSIVE CRYSTAL EMPIRE

The stunning Crystal Empire sparkles like a jewel!

Happy heart: A magical Crystal Heart helps to protect the Crystal Empire. The heart shoots a ribbon of pure energy up into the sky!

Dark times: Evil King Sombra once took over the Crystal Empire. He turned all the poor Crystal Ponies into slaves!

Sporting scene: The Crystal Empire has a huge sports arena that has enough room for many thousands of ponies. The Equestria Games have been held in this stadium.

Radiant rulers: Princess Cadance and Prince Shining Armor rule the Crystal Empire. They are wise, kind and very popular with all the ponies.

CRYSTAL HEART HUNT

Oh no! The Crystal Heart has gone missing. Can you find it in this sparkling scene? Once you've found the heart, award yourself a special heart sticker.

Turn to page 62 for the answer.

WHAT'S YOUR PONY PERSONALITY?

We know you'd be great pals with ALL the ponies, but which My Little Pony are you most like? Answer the questions below to find out which pony personality you share.

When you draw a picture, which of the following are you most likely to draw?

A A rainbow

B A book

C A bunny rabbit

D A bunch of balloons

What's your favourite game to play with your friends?

A Pretending to be racing drivers or pilots

B Making up stories

C Playing outside in the garden or park

D Running around as much as possible!

Your favourite outfit is . . .

A You don't care what you wear, as long as it's comfy!

B Something relaxed, like leggings and a T-shirt

C You always have a picture of a cute animal somewhere on your outfit

D You love to wear pink, sparkly, FUN outfits!

How would you describe yourself?

A Adventurous
B Creative
C Kind
D Funny

What's your favourite time of year?

A You love to be out and about in ALL the different seasons
B You like the winter, when you can wrap up warm and snuggle in front of a fire
C You love the springtime, when the baby animals are born
D You love the summer best, when the days are long

Which colour do you like best?

A Brilliant blue
B Calming purple
C Sunny yellow
D Bright pink

MOSTLY As

You are most like energetic, adventurous **RAINBOW DASH!** You just love being out and about and seeing lots of friends.

MOSTLY Bs

Your pony partner is terrific **TWILIGHT SPARKLE!** You are creative, kind and happy in your own company.

MOSTLY Cs

Your special pony friend is fabulous **FLUTTERSHY!** Just like this pretty pony, you are kind, generous and always look after your friends.

MOSTLY Ds

Your perfect pony pal is party-loving **PINKIE PIE!** Like Pinkie, you are a super-fun friend and full of good ideas. There is never a dull moment with you around!

Applejack's Crossword

How well do you know the world of the My Little Ponies? Test your knowledge by trying to complete Applejack's crossword.

2 A P P L E (3)

1 b o

4 B o g t e n d i s t a r s e

5 y e n

6 S P I C K

ACROSS

2 The element of harmony that Applejack represents

4 Where Pinkie Pie lives

6 The name of Twilight Sparkle's dragon assistant

DOWN

1 Princess Celestia's cutie mark symbol

3 The name of Rarity's little sister

5 The colour of Applejack's eyes

Turn to page 62 for the answers.

Princess Picture

Using your stickers, can you complete this gorgeous picture of Princess Twilight Sparkle? Use the picture at the top of the page as a guide.

The coldest outside temperature ever recorded is −89.2 °C in Antarctica. Brrrr!

Thunder is the sound we hear from a special sonic wave caused by air that has been rapidly heated by lightning. CRASH!

The sun is over one million times bigger than the Earth.

The largest hailstone ever recorded was the size of a football!

In a small village in Sri Lanka it once rained FISH! Scientists think that the fish were sucked up from the ocean by a swirling whirlwind and carried for a very long way.

You've heard of a rainbow, but what about a moonbow? These night-time rainbows are very rare. Light reflects off the surface of the moon, rather than the sun. Magical!

The city of Yuma, Arizona, is the sunniest on Earth with over 20 hours of sun a day.

RAINBOW DASH'S WACKY WEATHER

Rainbow Dash loves looking after the weather in Equestria! Here are her favourite weather facts from around the world.

Tempting Trail

Kind Fluttershy is looking forward to a treat! First find the stickers to fill the gaps, then choose the trail that leads Fluttershy to a yummy cake.

Turn to page 62 for the answer.

WONDERFUL WORDS

Twilight loves to spend her evenings playing word games with Spike and Owlowiscious. Can you work out the clues and untangle these ten animal anagrams? When you've finished, decorate the page with pretty animal stickers!

1

A baby or young pony.

ALOF

FOAL

2

Instead of feet, dogs and cats have these.

SWAP

PAWS

3

This eight-legged creature loves to spin webs.

PRIDES

SPIDER

4

This sea creature has lots of teeth!

HARSK

SHARK

5

This is a fish that looks more like a snake.

L E E

EEL

6

This night-time creature is said to be wise.

L O W

OWL

7

This striped animal is a close relative of the horse.

R A B E Z

_ _ _ _ _

8

These big-eared friends think carrots are yummy.

B A R B I T

Rabbit

9

This creature carries its home on its back!

A N S I L

SNAIL

10

These cuddly creatures make purr-fect pets.

A C T

cat

Turn to page 62 for the answers.

A Musical Farewell

You're almost at the end of the book! As a special farewell, your My Little Pony friends would like to share their favourite songs with you. These lyrics say a lot about the things that are most precious to them.

We're Apples for ever,
Apples together,

We're family, but so much more.

No matter what comes, we will face the weather,

We're Apples to the core!

A true, true friend helps a friend in need,

A friend will be there to help them see,

A true, true friend helps a friend in need,

To see the light that shines from a true, true friend!

Generosity, I'm here to show all that I can give,

Generosity, I'm here to set the bar,

Just sit back and watch how I live!

'Cause I love to make you smile, smile, smile,

It fills my heart with sunshine all the while,

'Cause all I really need's a smile, smile, smile,

From these happy friends of mine!

And when we come together,
Combine the light that shines within,
There is nothing we can't do,
There is no battle we can't win!

When we come together,
There'll be a star to guide the way,
It's inside us every day!

See it now! See it now!
Let the rainbow remind you,
That together we will always shine.
Let the rainbow remind you,
That, forever, this will be our time.

Why not try writing your own song all about something special to you?

and when me and charlotte
come togevurve hug. all
theeel all the timmme

Answers

Spike's Sparkly Search

In the Pony Know

1. B
2. B
3. A
4. C
5. B

Better Together

This lucky pony has a whole orchard full of these fruits!

In Twilight's house there are shelves full of these!

Some dragons hoard their treasure, but this little dragon eats these precious gems.

Pinkie Pie loves to make and eat these treats!

This cuddly creature is Fluttershy's best buddy.

Crystal Heart Hunt

Applejack's Crossword

```
                    1S
                     U
            2H O N E 3S T Y
                     W
                     E
                     E
                     T
   4S U 5G A R C U B E C O R N E R
      R              E
      E              B
      E              E
      N              L
                     L
                  6S P I K E
```

Tempting Trail

Wonderful Words

1. FOAL
2. PAWS
3. SPIDER
4. SHARK
5. EEL
6. OWL
7. ZEBRA
8. RABBIT
9. SNAIL
10. CAT

Explore the magical world of My Little Pony!

Orchard books are available from all good bookshops.
They can be ordered via our website: www.orchardbooks.co.uk,
or by telephone: 01235 827 702, or fax: 01235 827 703

ORCHARD

Spellbinding stories from My Little Pony!

Twilight Sparkle and the Crystal Heart Spell
by G. M. Berrow
978 1 40833 123 1

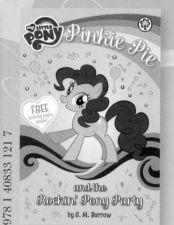

Pinkie Pie and the Rockin' Pony Party
by G. M. Berrow
978 1 40833 121 7

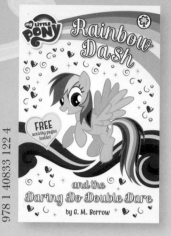

Rainbow Dash and the Daring Do Double Dare
by G. M. Berrow
978 1 40833 122 4

Rarity and the Curious Case of Charity
by G. M. Berrow
978 1 40833 704 2

Applejack and the Secret Diary Switcheroo
by G. M. Berrow
978 1 40833 695 3

Fluttershy and the Furry Friends Fair
by G. M. Berrow
978 1 40833 702 8

Princess Celestia and the Royal Rescue
by G. M. Berrow
978 1 40833 831 5

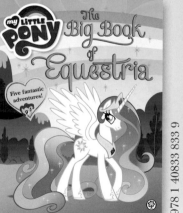

The Big Book of Equestria
Five fantastic adventures!
978 1 40834 461 3

Discord and the Ponyville Players
by G. M. Berrow
978 1 40833 833 9

Orchard books are available from all good bookshops.
They can be ordered via our website: www.orchardbooks.co.uk,
or by telephone: 01235 827 702, or fax: 01235 827 703

ORCHARD